PAINTBALL BLAST

BY JAKE MADDOX

illustrated by Sean Tiffany

text by Bob Temple

Librarian Reviewer
Chris Kreie
Media Specialist, Eden Prairie Schools, MN
MS in Information Media, St. Cloud State University, MN

Reading Consultant
Mary Evenson
Middle School Teacher, Edina Public Schools, MN
MA in Education, University of Minnesota

 **STONE ARCH BOOKS**
Minneapolis   San Diego

Impact Books are published by Stone Arch Books,
151 Good Counsel Drive, P.O. Box 669,
Mankato, Minnesota 56002
www.stonearchbooks.com

Library of Congress Cataloging-in-Publication Data
Maddox, Jake.
    Paintball Blast / by Jake Maddox; illustrated by Sean Tiffany.
    p. cm. — (Impact Books. A Jake Maddox sports story)
    Summary: When Max and Tyler start losing paintball matches to
a new player named Ryan, Max is suspicious and sets out to prove that
Ryan is cheating.
    ISBN-13: 978-1-59889-322-9 (library binding)
    ISBN-10: 1-59889-322-X (library binding)
    ISBN-13: 978-1-59889-417-2 (paperback)
    ISBN-10: 1-59889-417-X (paperback)
    [1. Paintball (Game)—Fiction. 2. Cheating—Fiction.] I. Tiffany,
Sean, ill. II. Title.
PZ7.M25643Pi 2007
[Fic]—dc22   2006027808

Art Director: Heather Kindseth
Graphic Designer: Kay Fraser

1 2 3 4 5 6 12 11 10 09 08 07

Printed in the United States of America.

TABLE OF CONTENTS

CHAPTER 1

CENTER STATION

Max Hauser leaped up from his hiding place and ran with everything he had. Hurdling over rocks and sticks, and dodging hanging branches, Max kept his head low as he ran. Then he heard it: Slap! Slap! SLAP!

Paintballs smacked into trees around him as he ran. He didn't feel anything hit him, so Max kept running. Then, finally, he made a dive for Center Station.

He made it. Max's chest heaved up and down as he sat inside Center Station. As he tried to catch his breath, Max checked himself. He needed to make sure he wasn't marked. He knew from experience that sometimes you could get marked on your clothes and never feel the hit.

Nothing. Max was free and clear. And now he was at Center Station, and that meant he was in control. The hidden shelter, which sat in the middle of the field, could give a person a view of almost any part of the field.

Max knew all about Center Station. After all, he had found it himself, and fixed it up with his friend Tyler. The field manager allowed them to build it right in the middle of the field.

Hidden by bushes and dug into the ground, Center Station was difficult to see. Some of the newer players didn't even know that it existed.

It started when Max found what looked like an old fort dug between some bushes in the middle of the field. Two wood walls and part of a roof remained. Another side was all dirt; it appeared that the fort had been built into the side of a hill. The other side was open all the way to the field.

Max and Tyler hid there a few times during their paintball matches, but it wasn't the best place. People coming in from the west could easily see in, and there were some good hiding places directly to the west. Max and Tyler sometimes felt like sitting ducks.

They had gone to the manager of the field and asked if they could fix it up. He had quickly agreed. Since then, Center Station had been a key lookout point for those who knew about it.

And now Max was there. He peered out through the lookout he and Tyler had built into the side of Center Station. He knew there were still two opponents out there, and that he was the only one on his team who had not been marked. It was all up to him.

He squinted as he used the lookout to see the field by the clubhouse. Nothing.

Sliding over on his seat, he managed to get a look to the east. Nothing there, either. Then he crawled across to look west.

Bingo. Leaning up against a wall, about fifty feet away and turned sideways to Max, was one of the two opponents. Max didn't know either boy. He just knew his goal was to mark them before they marked him.

Max pulled his marker up to his face and gazed through the sight. This would be easy. Slowly, carefully, Max squeezed the trigger. FOOM! The paintball left the marker. In a split second, there was an orange stain on his opponent's shoulder.

"Aw, shoot!" the boy yelled. "I'm marked!"

Just then, Max saw something move in the bush near the boy.

Must be his partner, Max thought.

He looked up and down, examining all the little branches for signs of clothing, glasses, anything. Then he saw it.

Pointing out through a bush, Max saw the barrel of a marker. Max knew from the angle of the barrel, he wasn't in danger.

It was pointed above his head. That guy must think I'm hiding in the bush above me, Max thought.

Max took aim. Based on where that barrel was pointed, he knew he could fire into that bush and mark the boy. Before he could pull the trigger, Max felt an unmistakable thump on his shoulder. He looked down. Sure enough, he was marked.

Max knew what he had to do. "I'm marked," he yelled. "I'm marked."

"We win!" came a cry from the bush.
"All right!"

Max sat in Center Station, staring at
the mark on his shoulder. How did this
happen? he thought. I know that barrel
was pointed over my head.

CHAPTER 2

SOMETHING'S NOT RIGHT

Max walked slowly back toward the clubhouse. His marker hung over his shoulder, bouncing against his side as he trudged along.

Up ahead, he saw the boy who marked him. He wasn't a boy Max recognized. The boy and his teammates were yelling and laughing. They jumped around and gave each other high fives.

Max wasn't upset about losing the match. He just couldn't figure out how it all happened. Max had been playing paintball for a couple of years. He had developed a good sense of when he was in trouble and when he wasn't. He didn't always win, but he was rarely fooled. This time, it just didn't feel right.

When Max reached the clubhouse, he bumped into Tyler. "Hey, Max," Tyler said. "What happened?"

"I don't know," Max said. "I saw him, saw the barrel of the marker, and it was pointed above my head. It looked like he was going to miss me by a mile. So I lined up the shot, and bang, it was over."

Tyler thought for a second. "That's strange," he said.

"What?" said Max.

"Well, I was just sitting in the lounge, and those two boys came in," Tyler said. "The taller one, the one that marked you, was talking to the assistant manager."

"Yeah? So what?" Max said.

"Well, he said something," Tyler said. "I didn't think it was strange at the time, but it sounds strange now."

"What did he say?"

"I heard the manager ask, 'Did it work?' Then the kid said, 'Yeah, worked like a charm.' I wonder if he tricked you somehow."

Max was silent. His face scrunched up as he thought about what Tyler said. "Tricked me?" Max said. "How could he have tricked me?"

"Maybe he had a fake barrel sticking out to distract you from the real one," Tyler said.

"No way, " Max said. "I know what I was looking at. I saw his hand on the marker. It was the marker that fired. There's no way he fooled me."

CHAPTER 3

FACE-TO-FACE

Max needed to find out what had happened during the game. It just didn't sit right with him. There was only one way to find out. He needed to ask the boy.

Max walked over to where the boy was standing. He was much bigger than Max — taller and stronger. He wore a yellow baseball cap backward. When Max approached, their conversation stopped.

"Hey," Max said. "Nice shot."

"Thanks," the boy said. He looked at his partner and smirked. "Good game."

There was an uncomfortable pause. Max wanted to keep the conversation going, but he didn't want to come right out and ask what the boy had done.

"I'm Max," he said. Max held out his hand.

"Ryan," the boy said, shaking Max's hand. "Ryan Weeks. This is Jay." Ryan motioned toward his friend.

Max kept the conversation going by asking questions about how long Ryan had been playing paintball and where he lived. He was surprised to learn that Ryan had just started playing.

"Wow," Max said. "You're pretty good, for just starting out."

"Aw, I just got lucky today," Ryan said. Again, he smirked at his friend.

Max felt bolder. "I almost had you, you know," he said. "I saw you in that bush. I mean, I saw the barrel of your marker. I was just getting ready to pull the trigger when I got marked."

"I figured," Ryan said. "But once you marked Jay, I knew where the shot came from, so I just fired."

Now Max was stumped. It sounded like Ryan was saying he didn't even see Max. He just fired in that direction and was lucky enough to hit him.

That would be one of the luckiest shots ever, Max thought. I was ducked down in Center Station. He could fire a hundred shots in that direction and still miss me.

Ryan quickly changed the subject. "Are you putting a team together for the Challenge Cup?" he asked. "It starts this Sunday."

Max wasn't sure what Ryan was talking about. "Haven't heard about it," Max said.

"They just announced it," Ryan said. "It's a big tournament. Six guys on a team. They're trying to get eight teams together for a tournament. You should get into it."

Max smiled. "I do a lot of two-man events with Tyler. We're a pretty good team. I think I could probably get six guys together to do it."

"Well, if you do," Ryan said, "I wouldn't hide in that bush again. I know now that's where you like to be." Ryan walked away, and Max's mouth dropped open.

He had been right all along — Ryan was aiming at the bush when he marked Max. But why, then, did his paintball go so low? Why did he miss his target and still get Max?

Just then, Tyler walked up. He saw the look of amazement on Max's face and immediately asked what was up.

"He cheated," Max said. "I don't know how, but I know he cheated."

"What? What are you talking about?" Tyler asked. The look on Max's face was full of determination.

"I'll tell you later," Max said. "Right now, we need to get a team for the Challenge Cup."

CHAPTER 4

GETTING READY

That night, Tyler came over to Max's house. Max told him what he had been thinking about Ryan.

"Look, I don't know how he did it," Max said. "I just know that he cheated. He admitted that he was shooting at the bush above Center Station. He still thinks I was behind it! So how did he aim so high and still get me?"

Neither boy could answer that question.

But they both knew that they wanted to find out. And they wanted to make sure they competed against Ryan in the Challenge Cup.

They spent much of the evening calling their friends who played paintball. They needed to pull together six players to compete in the event.

Eventually, they had all six players. The next morning, the boys went back to the paintball field.

As they approached the front counter, they saw the field manager, Bob, there. "Hey, guys," Bob said. "Are you going out to play today?"

"No, we're here to register for the Challenge Cup," Max said. "We've put a team together."

Bob grabbed the sign-up sheet. "That should be a fun event," he said. "That kid Ryan's team is going to be pretty tough."

Max nodded. "Yeah, we lost a match to Ryan and his friend yesterday," Max said. "It was some kind of lucky shot he marked me with."

Bob shook his head and laughed. "I don't know about that," he said.

"What do you mean?" said Max.

"Oh, I just know that he's a pretty good shooter," Bob said. "Since he's started playing paintball here, I don't think he's lost a match to anyone. It's amazing, really. When he first got here, he said he'd never played before. He must just be a natural."

"Or a cheater," Max said.

"What?" Bob said. He looked surprised. Max immediately wished he hadn't said anything. "Max, that's not like you," Bob said. "Just because someone is good, or he beats you, well, that doesn't mean he cheats."

"I know," Max said. "Let's just say I have my suspicions."

Max and Tyler turned to leave. Bob called out to them. "Doesn't matter anyway, Max," Bob said. "He won't be able to cheat in this tournament. We've got the rules set up, and we'll have officials out in the field watching all the matches."

Max led Tyler to the observatory area. The hallway windows overlooked much of the paintball field. As they walked along, Tyler noticed some kids out on the field playing.

"Hey, that's Ryan!" Tyler said.

Ryan was on the field. He had his back up against a big rock and was peering around it looking for an opponent. Tyler continued to walk down the hallway, out toward the parking lot.

"Hang on," Max said. "Let's watch for a minute. My mom won't be here for a couple of minutes."

The observatory was two stories above ground, so Max and Tyler had a pretty good view. Suddenly, Max saw one of Ryan's opponents streak across the field and dive behind a small hill. It was pretty clear that Ryan saw him too.

Ryan moved to a different part of the rock to get a better angle on the shot. "Watch him close," Max said.

They saw Ryan's opponent crawling along the ground. He moved three or four feet away from where he had been. Ryan clearly hadn't seen that movement; his aim never changed. Behind the glass, Max and Tyler couldn't hear the action. What they saw amazed them.

Ryan fired his marker in the direction of the hill.

A second later, the opponent stood up. He was at least three feet to the left of where Ryan had shot. And he had a small yellow mark on his shirt.

Ryan raised his arms in triumph.

Game over.

CHAPTER 5

OPENING ROUND

Max and Tyler rode together to their first match in the Challenge Cup. All the way there, the boys talked about what they had seen.

Tyler wasn't sure what to think about what happened to Max on the paintball field the day before. Now that he had seen Ryan in action, however, Tyler agreed that something was up.

"Do you think he might just have a bad marker, one that doesn't shoot straight?" Tyler said. "I mean, that's possible, right?"

"I guess," Max said. "But Bob said Ryan has never lost. If he had a bad marker, he'd miss all kinds of shots. He wouldn't be able to aim."

Tyler nodded. They rode the rest of the way in silence.

When they arrived at the field, they immediately went into the clubhouse to see who their opponent would be.

The tournament schedule was posted on the wall. Max and Tyler had named their team the Marks Brothers. Their first opponent would be the Blue Devils.

The boys scanned the list of teams. Ryan's team was called the Red Menace.

Based on the tournament setup, the Red Menace wouldn't meet up with Max and Tyler's team unless both teams made it to the championship match.

The Red Menace's first match was just ending as Max and Tyler headed down toward the field and started to put on all their gear.

Ryan passed Tyler and Max on their way to the field. Ryan looked pretty happy.

"Did you win?" Max asked.

"Of course," Ryan said. "Wouldn't have it any other way."

A few seconds later, a couple of members of the other team walked by. They each were marked with yellow paint.

Max shook his head.

Before Max could say anything to Ryan, the official called the Marks Brothers over for a talk.

Max and the Blue Devils' captain listened carefully to the rules.

There were four bases set up in the four corners of the huge field. The teams would draw for their base. To start the match, each team would begin at its base. A horn would sound, and the teams could spread out as they wished. The goal was to mark every member of the opposing team. A marked player had to leave the field. Whichever team marked the entire other team first was the winner.

"You can use any marker you have," the official said. "The club will provide the paintballs." The official pointed at a table that included the boxes of paintballs.

Max's team would use pink balls in the first round, and the Blue Devils would use green balls.

Max and Tyler quickly made a plan. They talked with their teammates about how they would spread out from the west base, their starting point. They would try to push toward the middle of the field. The goal was to get Max to Center Station, where he could use his shooting skills to protect the rest of the team and mark the opponents.

The horn sounded to start the match. The Marks Brothers fanned out around the field. Max stayed toward the back. As the team moved forward, Max moved farther from behind. Shortly after the match started, Tyler saw a couple of members of the Blue Devils hiding behind a tree.

Tyler took aim and marked the first player. As the second one scampered toward a different location, Tyler marked him, too. He signaled to Max with two fingers, then pointed down to the ground, meaning "Two down."

It took about a half hour before the Blue Devils were down to their last player. Max had marked one of them, and the other four were marked by other members of the Marks Brothers team. Max and Tyler were the only ones left on their team. They were in control; Max had made it to Center Station.

Tyler pursued the last Blue Devils player. Every time he moved to a new location, Tyler used the opportunity to get behind him. He tried to force the Blue Devils player toward Center Station.

It worked perfectly. Tyler moved around behind the opponent. He got off a couple of shots, but missed them both. The shots told the player where Tyler was shooting from, however. As he tried to move farther away from Tyler, he was actually moving closer to Max in Center Station.

At last, Max had him in his sights. The boy was looking back toward Tyler, and Max had a clear shot from the side.

He aimed and fired, marking the boy on his leg.

The match was over. Max and Tyler were one step closer to a showdown with Ryan.

CHAPTER 6

The semifinal matches were scheduled
for the next weekend. Max and Tyler
met a couple of times during the week to
talk about their strategy. Every time, they
ended up talking about Ryan. They were
more suspicious than ever.

Ryan's team had its semifinal match
right before the Marks Brothers' match.
Max and Tyler wanted to see it. They made
plans to watch it from the observatory.

All week long, the boys talked about the matches. They couldn't get the tournament out of their minds. The weekend couldn't come fast enough.

When Saturday morning finally arrived, the boys were anxious and ready. They gathered up their gear and headed for the paintball field. They arrived just in time for the start of Ryan's match with the other team.

The two teams were already out on the field. Max and Tyler hurried to the observatory. They saw Ryan right away.

He was stalking along the fence line, near the clubhouse. Ryan made a quick run along the fence, then cut toward the middle of the field.

He dove behind a rock just in time to miss getting marked.

Most of the rest of the action was going on farther out in the field. It was hard for Max and Tyler to see much of it from the observatory. Ryan kept working his way toward the middle of the field. Max thought he might be heading for Center Station, but Ryan never got there.

Gradually, they saw a few of the opposing team's players walking in. They had been marked. The yellow blotches on their clothing told the story. Max and Ryan kept track as the players came in. After an hour or so, Ryan was the only member of his team left. There were three players still going on the other team.

"He's going down this time," Tyler said.

"I hope he doesn't," Max said. "I want to go against him in the finals."

The action was getting closer to the observatory. Max and Tyler could see a little more of what was happening.

Ryan was hiding between two bushes down to the left. There were two opponents ahead of him, hiding a few feet apart behind separate barricades. The third player was behind Ryan. Max and Tyler were pretty sure Ryan couldn't see him.

The two boys in front of Ryan were trying to communicate to each other but appeared to be having trouble.

One went over to the other, joining him behind a barricade. Ryan saw the boy move. He crawled along to a better location and lined up his shot.

Max and Tyler saw Ryan shoot.

In a matter of a few seconds, both of the guys on the field stood up. They had been marked! A split second later, the third boy charged up from behind. He scooted along the wall right under the observatory. Tyler and Max saw Ryan notice him. Ryan spun quickly and fired toward the boy.

The next thing Max and Tyler saw was Ryan raising his hands over his head. He had won!

CHAPTER 7

EVIDENCE

Max turned to Tyler. "Did you see what just happened?" Max asked.

"Yeah," Tyler said. "That was amazing. He marked three guys in about two seconds. Maybe he really is that good!"

"No," said Max. "He marked three guys with two shots. TWO shots. How's that even possible?"

Tyler looked confused. "How do you know he only shot twice?" he asked.

"Weren't you watching?" Max said. "He shot once at the barricade, and once toward the wall. I'm telling you, there's something fishy going on here."

Max and Tyler headed down toward the field. They passed the three boys Ryan had marked. Each of them had a small yellow blotch on their clothing.

Max and Tyler finished putting their gear on and marched out to the field.

Max walked along the wall under the observatory. There, on the wall, he saw two yellow blotches. "Tyler, come here!" Max said. "Look at the wall. There's two more spots on it from Ryan's shot!"

Tyler didn't look sure. "How do you know they were from Ryan? Those could have been up there for weeks."

Max walked to the wall. He reached out his finger and touched one of the spots. As he dragged his finger down the wall, a yellow line trailed behind it. The paint was still wet.

"I think his marker fires more than one paintball at a time," Max said.

"If that's true, we have to tell Bob," Tyler said, shaking his head.

Before the boys could make a move, a whistle blew. It was time to start their match. The protest would have to wait.

Out on the field, Max wasn't able to help his team much. He was too distracted. His mind wandered. He tried to figure out how Ryan was doing it. Tyler and a couple of the other boys were able to mark three of the opponents.

Finally, Max's daydreaming got him into trouble. He suddenly found himself surrounded. Three members of the other team had formed a triangle around him.

They were about sixty feet away, but Max knew they were there. His only hope was that one of his teammates would mark one of them. That would create an opening for him to escape. Max decided to lie still between a bush and a barricade, hoping he wouldn't be seen.

A long time passed. Max still felt like he was trapped. But since no one had tried to mark him, he thought the boys might have moved away.

Max decided to try to crawl to safety. As soon as he turned over to begin moving, he felt it. SLAP! A paintball hit him square in the side. He was marked!

Max stood up and took off his goggles. The match was over for him. Now it was up to Tyler and the other boys to win it. The match lasted for more than an hour.

It was tough for Max to watch from the observatory without being able to help. Finally, Tyler marked the last member of the other team. They were in the finals!

Only one problem remained — making sure the match would be fair.

CHAPTER 8

LOOKING FOR HELP

Max marched into the clubhouse and found Bob. He tried to explain the evidence that he had against Ryan.

Max told Bob about the conversation Tyler had overheard, when Ryan said that something had "worked like a charm." He told Bob about watching from the observatory, when Ryan shot to the left and still marked the player. He explained that Ryan had marked three players with two shots.

Finally, he told Bob about the shot that ended Ryan's semifinal match — the single shot that marked a player and put two stains on the wall.

Bob shook his head. "Max, you've got to let this go," he said. "It's all in your imagination. For some reason, you've decided that Ryan is a bad kid. He's not. He's just another paintball player like you, and he happens to be very good at it."

Max asked about the markers. He wanted to know if Ryan could be using a special marker of some kind.

"Max, you know we inspect the markers before each match," Bob said. "Ryan's team isn't using an illegal marker."

"What about the balls?" Max said. "Could he be using a special paintball?"

"Max, let me ask you a question," Bob said. "Where did you get the paintballs for your two matches?"

"From the official," Max said. He sighed. He knew what Bob was getting at.

"Yeah, the same place where Ryan got his," Bob said. "We supply all the paintballs for the event."

"Okay, okay," Max said. He still wasn't satisfied that Ryan wasn't cheating. But it seemed like he was running out of ways to prove it. "Will you just come down to the field and look at the marks on the wall?"

The marks had dried by the time Max and Bob got to them. Bob looked at them, but there wasn't much he could say.

"They were both wet right after their match," Max said.

"How do you know he didn't shoot three times?" Bob said.

"He marked three boys in about three seconds," Max said. "If he had taken three shots to mark them, and marked the wall twice, that's five shots in three seconds. It's impossible!"

Bob sighed. "Look, Max," he said. "If it will make you feel better, I will personally inspect all of the gear for the final match myself and make sure nobody's got any hidden markers or paintballs in their clothing, either."

"Okay," Max said. "Thanks, Bob."

That night, Max went home. He was sure that Ryan was cheating with special paintballs or markers. But he knew he couldn't prove it.

Max turned on his computer and got on the Internet. He searched for paintball markers and found tons of different kinds. None of them seemed to explain what Ryan was doing. Then Max searched for special paintballs. There wasn't much to be found there, either.

Finally, Max typed "triple paintball" into his search engine. One link appeared. Max clicked it quickly. Up popped a Web page advertising "TripleBlast Three-ball Paintballs."

It read:

"TripleBlast Three-ball Paintballs are a revolution in high-powered paintball play. Surprise your opponents with triple the marking power. Just one shot produces three tiny paintballs! Now you can mark opponents you can't even see."

Max couldn't believe what he was reading. At the bottom of the page, in very small type, it said, "Available only in fluorescent yellow."

Immediately, Max knew what he had to do. He printed the page. Then he sent an instant message to Tyler with a link to the site. They talked about how they could prove it to Bob that Ryan was using the TripleBlast paintballs.

There was only one question left. How was Ryan getting the balls?

CHAPTER 9

SHOWDOWN

The next Saturday was showdown day.
Max and Tyler's Marks Brothers team was
set to play against Ryan's Red Menace for
the championship of the Challenge Cup.

Both teams arrived early. Max went
straight to Bob's office, but he wasn't there.
Max left the printout from the Web site
on Bob's desk. Then he headed out to the
playing field.

The teams met separately to talk about strategy. Max and Tyler worked out the plan with their team. Again, the idea would be to get Max to Center Station. He could control the match from there.

Max couldn't wait to get started. When the official called the captains together, both teams came running in. Bob was there to keep an eye on things.

"Okay, everyone," Bob said. "To make sure we are going to have a fair match, I'm going to check everyone out. I need to make sure no one has extra markers or paintballs."

Max expected Ryan to get upset, but Ryan just smiled. He didn't seem to mind the inspection.

Bob didn't find anything suspicious.

The captains drew for their starting positions. Max drew the west base. Ryan drew the north base. Then the official handed out the paintballs.

"Marks Brothers, you will have purple today," he said. "Red Menace, you will have yellow."

"Yellow again?" Max blurted out. Ryan glared back at him. "They sure get yellow a lot," Max added quietly.

The teams grabbed their boxes of paintballs and headed to their bases. Before long, the match was underway.

The Marks Brothers fanned out and began to move slowly toward the center of the field. Before they could get very far, three Red Menace players came charging out from behind some branches.

Two of the Marks Brothers players were taken by surprise. They were both quickly marked, and all three of the Red Menace players found cover safely.

Max saw the whole thing happen. Two men down already! Both of those boys had been to the left side. That meant the Marks Brothers team was weak there. Instead of hanging back behind the rest, Max moved to the left to keep the team fanned out.

The three Red Menace players moved off toward the right. None of the other Red Menace players were in sight. Gradually, Max moved along the outside of the field. He kept his back to the outer fence. That way, no one could sneak up behind him.

Max tried to stay low. Sometimes, if he felt others were nearby, he even crawled.

Suddenly, Max saw a Red Menace player rush up behind a rock that was about twenty-five feet away. Max had a pretty clear view of the boy, so he took aim. SLAP! One shot, and the boy was marked.

Now Max was worried that he had given away his location by firing. He tried to crawl silently away. Then he heard a rustling in the bushes to his right. Max knew he was in trouble. He popped up and ran quickly, keeping his head low.

"Gotcha!" he heard a voice cry. It was Ryan. Then, SMACK! He heard a paintball hit the fence behind him. Max dove for the ground. He rolled to his back to see if he was hit. Still safe. Then he shot a glance at the wall. There, as plain as could be, were three small yellow splats.

Max smiled. He knew he had Ryan now. He also knew he was still in trouble. Quickly, he crawled to the nearest barricade and slipped in. It was the north base! The Red Menace's box of paintballs was there.

Max opened it quickly. Inside were several smaller boxes of paintballs. One of the boxes was not like the others. On the side it said "TripleBlast." Max rushed to open it. It was empty. Thinking quickly, Max folded the box up and stuffed it in a pocket. He would need it for evidence later.

Max still had one more piece of business to take care of. He had to mark Ryan. Max bolted from the north base and rolled behind a rock. He spotted Tyler behind a barricade.

Using hand signals, Tyler told Max that only Ryan was left from the other team.

Max gave Tyler a sign to use the plan they agreed to do. Tyler understood. From behind his barricade, Tyler made a little bit of noise. Then he fired his marker toward where Ryan was hiding. Tyler wasn't trying to hit Ryan. He was trying to show Ryan where he was.

Ryan sensed where Tyler was from the activity. Ryan crawled out from behind a rock and propped up his elbows on it to take aim. Tyler made a little more noise.

Max saw a grin move across Ryan's face. Max glanced across at Tyler and gave a signal. Tyler rushed across the field. Ryan easily marked him. It didn't matter.

Ryan's shirt now had a bright purple stain on it. Max had marked him.

Before Max and Tyler could even celebrate their victory, they saw Bob talking to Ryan. The boys walked over. Bob was taking Ryan's marker and his paintballs. As the boys approached, Ryan walked slowly away.

"Thanks for the printout, Max," Bob said. "I watched the match from the observatory. When I saw the three marks on the wall, I knew what was happening. I did a little checking in the locker where we keep the paintballs. I found a big box of these TripleBlast balls. Turns out my assistant was sneaking them to Ryan in their paintball supply."

A moment later, Bob handed over the Challenge Cup trophy to Max, Tyler, and their team. They'd won — fair and square.

ABOUT THE AUTHOR

Bob Temple lives in Rosemount, Minnesota, with his wife and three children. He has written more than thirty books for children. Over the years, he has coached more than twenty soccer, basketball, and baseball kids' teams. He also loves visiting classrooms to talk about his writing.

ABOUT THE ILLUSTRATOR

When Sean Tiffany was growing up, he lived on a small island off the coast of Maine. Every day, from sixth grade until he graduated from high school, he had to take a boat to get to school. When Sean isn't working on his art, he works on a multimedia project called "OilCan Drive," which combines music and art. He has a pet cactus named Jim.

GLOSSARY

barrel (BARE-uhl)—the long part of a marker, from which the paintball flies

barricade (BARE-uh-kade)—a barrier that is used to stop people or things from going past a certain point

marker (MARK-ur)—the piece of equipment used to shoot paintballs

observatory (uhb-ZUR-vuh-tor-ee)—a place from which you can watch something

officials (uh-FISH-uhls)—the people who enforce the rules of a game in sports

opponent (uh-POH-nuhnt)—the person or team that is against you in a fight or game

semifinal (SEM-ee-FYE-nuhl)—the match or game that determines which individual or team plays in the final

strategy (STRAT-uh-jee)—a plan

tournament (TUR-nuh-muhnt)—a series of contests or games

MORE PAINTBALL GAMES

CAPTURE THE FLAG: This is a very common game. Two teams are formed and each team hides or posts a flag. The object is to get the other team's flag, without getting marked, and before they capture your team's flag.

CENTER FLAG: Similar to Capture the Flag, except that there is just one flag in the middle of the playing field. The object is to get the flag before the other team does, and take it back to your team's base without getting marked.

SAVE THE KING: Two or more teams play. Each team chooses one player to be its leader. Teams must protect their leader while trying to mark the other team's leader. The game ends when only one leader remains.

BUNNY HUNT: One player (the "bunny") goes into the field. All the other players attempt to mark that player before they are marked. This is a great game, especially if you have one player who is more experienced than all the others. He or she should be the bunny.

FREEZE TAG: Two teams play. When a player is marked, he or she stands in place. The marked player can become active again if he or she is tagged by a teammate. Therefore, opponents must "guard" players who have been marked. One team wins when all members of the other team have been marked.

DISCUSSION QUESTIONS

1. What do you think would have happened if Max had confronted Ryan about his cheating when he first suspected it?

2. In what other ways could Max have proved that Ryan was cheating?

3. If you were heading into a competition of some kind, and you knew your opponent was going to cheat, what would you do?

4. Why do you think Max decided to go ahead with the match, instead of refusing to play against a cheater?

WRITING PROMPTS

1. Max couldn't get Bob to believe his story about Ryan's cheating. Write about a time in your life when you couldn't get important people to believe something that was true.

2. How would you have tried to prove that Ryan was cheating?

3. Have you ever accused someone of doing something that they didn't do? Write about what it felt like to realize you were wrong.

INTERNET SITES

Do you want to know more about subjects related to this book? Or are you interested in learning about other topics? Then check out FactHound, a fun, easy way to find Internet sites.

Our investigative staff has already sniffed out great sites for you!

Here's how to use FactHound:

1. Visit *www.facthound.com*

2. Select your grade level.

3. To learn more about subjects related to this book, type in the book's ISBN number: **159889322X**.

4. Click the **Fetch It** button.

FactHound will fetch the best Internet sites for you!